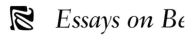 *Essays on Be*

CW01072813

Essays on
Being Alive

Raymond Johnston

Celtic Cat Publishing

Knoxville, Tennessee

LIMITED 2006 EDITION

First published in 2006
by Celtic Cat Publishing, Knoxville,
Tennessee, in association with centredself.
www.celticcatpublishing.com
www.centredself.com

After reading this book you may feel that you
would like to support the work of St. John's
Hospice. You may do so by sending donations to
St. John's Hospice, Slyne Road, Lancaster LA2 6ST,
United Kingdom or in the U.S.A. to St. John's
Hospice, c/o Celtic Cat Publishing, 2654 Wild
Fern Lane, Knoxville, TN 37931

ISBN: 0-9658950-8-4
Library of Congress Control Number: 2005938855

This book is dedicated to Dr. Margaret Ellam, the finest of physicians, and all the staff, St. John's Hospice, Lancaster; to Susan Aitken, psychologist, who opened my eyes and my mind; and, most of all, to Jane, Rory and Anna, whose unconditional love called me back to life.

It is not true
that death begins after life.
When life stops
death also stops.

—Gösta Ågren (1)

. . . for what would be
the point of anything,
if nothing is remembered?

—Drosoula remembers Philothei in
Louis de Bernières *Birds Without Wings* (2)

 *Preface*

Memory and Meaning

What's it all about?

Here is an image of life. Intimations of immortality are everywhere. We are surrounded by structures, imposing and enduring; by edifices, rituals and norms that induce comfort and sensations of permanence, continuity and security. We accumulate, garner and institutionalise yet we must know all is fleeting and ephemeral. Inevitably and inescapably we are naked, no matter how we choose to dress up life.

Here is another image. We are seduced by dualism, by dark and light, by one or other. Yet our world is much richer in texture and subtle in shade. There are oceans of distinctions between and beyond the sacred and the sensual, sickness and health, loving and loathing, truth and lies, dependency and autonomy, change and inertia, illusion and epiphany. Most likely, one will be in bed with the other, offering a myriad of possibilities in the way we come to terms with the lives we lead.

If we listen, we detect an incessant, erratic, unsettling murmur within the steady pulse of our existence.

Depending on your point of view, such ideas are simply examples of man's deeper existential consciousness or his appreciation of the 'mysteries' of life. They are to do with our own sense of mortality and vulnerability when set against the immensity of our cosmic universe. We become aware of how nothing is quite as it appears to be. We sense the fault lines in our own make-up, the imperfections, the built in obsolescence. Yet, however tiny our portion in time and however minuscule our impact on history, each of us makes an extraordinary, detailed universe of our own, in which we are the main actor within a network of friends, family and colleagues. We see excellence in others and wonder; we mourn the mediocre in ourselves. But we need to celebrate, whatever our little triumphs. Each of us would like, at least, to leave a footprint, however quickly washed away.

Shot to pieces

It doesn't take much to shake the equilibrium of our lives. Any little shock will do it, enough to set mind and emotions racing. Loss is one of those shocks — loss of a job, loss of a friendship, loss of a loved one through death or loss of our health through serious illness. Their velocity and intensity may be sufficient to throw our larger lives into total disarray. And we don't heal quickly.

Even while we may imagine we have our heads back in order, it may be a long time before the turbulent waves of our emotions settle down. No doubt it's hard to value any pain — but at least it tells us we are alive. Paradox and contradiction may be disturbing, but they also may be the most compelling drivers within our lives, injecting vitality where there is dullness or complacency, apathy or lethargy.

Another image of life is that it is cyclical. This is the image most often used to symbolise the passing of seasons or the process of birth, life, death and resurrection. In *As You Like It* Shakespeare propels us through the ages of man, returning us in old age to an infant-like state of dependency. Modern psychology helps us gain insight into our lives by working the same theme — but this time in a much more dynamic way. Take Robert Hobson. In his wonderful *Forms of Feeling: The Heart of Psychotherapy,* he repeatedly reminds us that 'Growing up is a cycle of loss, relative disorganisation, and reorganisation. Loss is associated with fear . . .' and later 'Anxiety and fear lie at the heart of existence. . . . In growing up we are faced again and again with the pain of mourning: of loss, disorganisation, and reorganisation'. (3)

Somehow, in some way, we have to make sense of all these persistent threads that weave through the progress of our lives — the ambiguity, the complexity, the vulnerability. 'Our life stories, and those of our families and communities', says Thomas Attig, 'are filled with the weaving and reweaving of webs of connection, patterns of caring within which we find and make meaning'. Loss, serious illness, bereavement shatter those comforting patterns. 'Much of the weaving that comprises our individual and collective life histories is undone'. The cycle again — 'As we relearn the worlds of our experience, we reweave the fabric of our lives and come to a new wholeness'. (4)

Catch me, if you can

The shock of loss is at its most devastating when we are faced with the loss of life — either our own or of someone very close to us. Such is the intensity that it is sometimes impossible to cope with all the currents of emotion on our own. How can we understand this level of loss? Perhaps the starting point is an attempt at empathy; to remember something of moments when fear or panic gripped us in everyday life and then extrapolate. Imagine what it might be like to live with such anxiety and fear as a constant gut-wrenching sensation through day and night, day after day, night after night. That's how to come close.

Being close to someone who is ill or dying can be demanding and unsettling. How difficult to be dispassionate when their aching vulnerability exposes our own! Most often the physical needs for support and care are most apparent and, however draining, the easiest to meet.

What we are less prepared for may be the exposure of raw emotion, fear and dread. What we know is that a physical crisis most often produces internal disarray. This is less easy to deal with and may be avoided by carers for fear that they will say the wrong thing or even increase the distress. Perhaps our courage 'to be bold' may be strengthened if we are able to understand a bit more about what it is like to be critically or chronically ill. What happens to us when there is an existential 'shock' to our system? What emotional crises burst through the fault lines to the surface of our lives? What is it like to experience 'disintegration' — and what can any of us do to assist the rebuilding and 'reorganisation'?

It is clear that physical trauma usually leads to mental and emotional upheaval; serious illness can take us to 'the brink' and thereby produce an existential crisis. Certainly, this is a very sensitive and often emotionally charged area of human experience. Illness often induces fundamental questioning and a crying need for affirmation about what has been and what might be. Individuals who are ill often come to see their past and present in a very different light; 'importances' get rearranged. A carer may be the most precious companion on that last part of life's journey. Catch me, if you can.

Talking about life

Having been in and out of St. John's Hospice regularly as an inpatient and day-care patient over an 18 month period, I became very aware of just how much we all need to talk — or rather, be listened to. It would seem that precariousness and anxiety increase our need to be heard. Certainly the prospect of death provokes a different perspective on life. Talking allows us to register that we are still here, still functioning. By its very nature, existential torment is so difficult to get on top of; it is as if we are consumed by it. We cannot step outside the intensity of the experience to see our way through it. We have no distance. And distance is everything. It is hard to see clearly without it. The best carers are those who know this.

At the Hospice, staff know how to listen. They can recognise elementary signs of sadness and distress and gently open the door, that felt tightly shut, to a conversation. They make the space and time to come alongside, enabling patients to 'talk out' the feelings that have surfaced through their physical breakdown. They are able to help patients find the words, put things back in perspective, rediscover courage, and repair their shattered sense of self. In doing these things, above all, they help patients to restore a sense of meaning, value and significance in their lives.

But hold on, isn't this the preserve of a priest or a psychologist you might say? I don't think so. Actually, it's what good friends do every day. We just don't think of it in those terms. Yes, the conversations are better if they are undertaken with an awareness of what a patient might need or be going through. Certainly, they are more productive if there is empathy. But think of it — this is the ground on which we all walk; this is our shared human experience, issues faced by all carers in their lives and not just the province of the professional. Universal themes, individual experiences.

Having observed the team in St. John's at work (and experienced their care myself) I have learned something of what might matter to someone who is critically ill. I will speak of the impact on myself but with the knowledge that these issues were deeply important to most of those I have had the privilege to meet as fellow patients. Six elements of conversation seem to matter very much.

Affirmation matters. This happens in any human interaction when carers 'attend' totally — not with just half a brain in gear and the other half absorbed in other commitments, pressures or interests — and is reflected most obviously in body language. But it was transmitted most powerfully to me in words of positive encouragement and recognition of what I was going through. It helped me appreciate just how far I had come and how much I had accomplished through the course of my illness.

Biography matters. This provided the opportunity, and permission, to talk about my own story, which at times I was desperate to do. It helped me to remember and clarify personal history that sometimes got terribly confused, with all its ups and downs, humour, tragedy and turning points, enabling me to restore a coherent and cohesive sense of myself that I could value and be proud of.

Significance matters. Here I was helped to identify and reflect on the defining moments within my personal story that represented the best of my life. In this way I was given something precious to hold on to. But less pleasant areas were not avoided if I needed to talk about them — significance can also be about articulation of concerns — be they unfinished business, regrets, unresolved feelings that I needed to clear out from within my own head. And, of course, time mattered. As the conversations unfolded, I became very aware that the story was not yet over and that I yearned for whatever was left to be full of the things I valued most — dignity, courage, generosity and love.

Personal resourcefulness matters. I had to be helped to find my courage that I had lost along the way, and the determination and motivation to continue. I felt able to use my personal history as a resource in such a way that I became more able to rediscover those attributes and experiences from my past life that could help me cope with the situation now. The carers were able to listen to the feelings behind my words and help me recognise and acknowledge my own puzzlement, delight, annoyance or whatever — and determine whether there was any issue that I wanted to do something about.

Perspective matters. The enormity of serious illness naturally leads to a very strong focus on the self (nothing particularly wrong with that!) — but sometimes it was helpful to be able to step beyond the immediate confinement of my feelings and discover a wider context within which I could place myself in relation to others who mattered to me. So the best of the carers were able to help me think through the potential ongoing impact of my illness on others.

Decision making matters. The ultimate freedom — to be able to choose 'how to be' in relation to anything that confronts us. It mattered to me to regain some sense of personal power, to move from victim status, to feel that there was room for manoeuvre, particularly in regard to how I chose to behave and react to any new set of circumstances that now confronted me. The exercise of that freedom itself propelled me into a better place.

Recognise these? Yes, of course. In talking about these things we are talking about the life that we all know. These are what lie at the heart of each of our journeys through life, often taken for granted, sometimes suppressed, frequently overlooked and maybe only surfacing when loss demands a reappraisal of who and where we are. It is the wise and sensitive carer who is alert to these real concerns, for these are likely to be at the core of the emotions, distress, fear and apprehension that erupt through the fragments of our physical selves when we become so depleted. Those who are really ill may need a companion on that particular journey — and we need to be bold enough as carers to go there in the confidence that this is where we would want to be ourselves if the situation was reversed.

Memories are made of this

Thomas Attig says 'Remembering is not a retreat to the past. Rather memory brings aspects of the past into present awareness. We attend to and cherish their legacies here and now'. (5)

Experience of illness tells me this is so. As we 'reorganise' we use whatever building blocks come to hand. Memories are corner stones that help give shape and form to our new reality. Significantly, they are not about recreating the past. Most often, that cannot return. But they do give us a measure of how things have changed or are changing, yet preserving the values and meaning that we wish to build into whatever time is left to us. So, incredibly, memory can help us interpret the data coming at us in our present experience, however disturbing.

Of course, memories can be troubling, for they reawaken moments of embarrassment, lapses of judgement, inappropriate reactions, short lived passions and muddled motivations. But interestingly, in spite of this, they may temper the drift to nostalgia or sentimentality. At their best, they keep us grounded, remind us of the reality of our human condition. Like suffering, they are part of the make up of all our lives and a key part of that cycle of learning . . . that is if we are able to face them and reflect and choose a better way to be.

The importance of this is that there are likely to be many powerful dynamics at play (in the life of the person who is ill or dying) that are not immediately to do with the illness but that surface because of it. These have a major bearing on how well each of us is able to handle what is going on. In normal life, context governs the wholeness of most interactions. In illness it is all too easy to focus down on the immediacy of the presenting physical conditions and miss what may be of most importance to the patient. Thankfully, palliative care attempts to treat the person 'as a whole'. That means working at whatever levels are necessary for the patient to have the best shot, with the optimum quality of life possible, with a range of caring approaches. Caring, at its best, is about the life yet to be lived and that is impossible without support for the inner journey.

Being Alive

The essays which follow, titled 'Being Alive', were written over 18 months of serious, life threatening illness. They illustrate what happens when real care is taken and have evolved because of conversations such as I have described above. They are about the joy of life — life that is inclusive of suffering as a normal and expected part.

I suspect most people have a 'Being Alive' inside them. They may not write it down or articulate it in the same way. They may use photographs as a springboard. They may even rehearse with a carer what they really want to say to a loved one, but haven't been able to. They may delight in remembering moments of true pleasure and achievement. They may talk of wrongs to be righted — or at least of the desire to say sorry. They may ponder over unfinished business and messages to send where they haven't been able to find the right words or right moment in the past. They may have disappointments that they simply want to have acknowledged. And they may need to record what they made of the time that they had and whisper about moments of quiet heroism within their own lives. Each, a footprint, however quickly to be washed away.

All of a sudden I understand a true legacy to be that part of myself that I can leave behind. This gift may be symbolic, it may be recorded in some way, but essentially it inspires memories that have meaning, meaning that endures beyond the time that I have.

October 2005

🅡 *Being Alive*

Adventures and conquests

◙ *One*

Recently I have developed a compelling interest in being alive. Perhaps this is because I lingered too long on death's precipitous edge, drawn to its generously proffered gift of unending silence. Only reluctantly, it seems, did I turn the other way towards a narrow path, hard and roughly hewn.

Of course, in some sense I never made the choice. It 'happened' to me, as if blown by a prevailing wind through fear, guilt, panic, encouragement and compulsion, eventually steeling my resolve.

It seems clear that being alive only makes sense in the light of being dead. The source of our will and drive resides here and the imperative to make something of what we have. We are alerted to the passing of time and the measure of significance. We are helped to appreciate the distinctive character of anything by its opposite, or by its contrast. We apprehend and appreciate day because of night, hard because of soft, love because of loss, existence because of non-existence.

But being alive is much, much more than mere existence. The endeavour to discover what it might be comes rather late in the day for me. This doesn't mean that I never tasted life in all its vibrancy and colour before. It's just that, in taking it for granted, blinding myself to the fact that it wouldn't always be there, I drank too hastily and omitted to savour the moments to the depth and extent that I could have. So, when the crisis came, there was a desperately depleted reservoir from which to draw.

I haven't made the most of my days. I have spent too much time getting somewhere else rather than really investing in where I am now. Every so often, a disturbing thought would pierce my complacency, like a little electric shock. Why did I sometimes feel so frustrated in what I was doing? Did I place value on something principally because it seemed important to someone else? In truth, was the value measured in personal gain, status or financial reward? And what about the alternatives set aside? Could they be justified or rationalised so easily; the friends neglected, the relationships drifting away, the tasks unfinished, the promises unfulfilled?

So what is 'being alive'? Years ago my philosophy professor would confront my mental lethargy with the distinction between living and existing. With a devilish twinkle in his eyes, he would take students to the edge of a field to watch cows grazing, chewing cud, slowly regurgitating and masticating grass. 'Is this living or existing'? he would ask. The intervening years have not dimmed the profound implications of such apparently simple questioning. There was no implied diminution of the condition of cattle. They are as they are. But there was a persistent if patient confrontation of what I was in myself and, consequently, what I was choosing to do with my life, my mind, my time. There was an urgent call to understand more about what was real or fact or certainty.

I now appreciate just how much a quality of life depends on being 'inside' the living experience rather than passing through it, oblivious to so much of what is really going on, or escaping in daydreams and fantasy. Essentially this means staying alert in order to stay alive — training oneself to attend more, to recognise more, to notice more and appreciate more, whether landscape or people, objects or ideas. That passion for alertness needs to extend to the self as well — the immediate recognition of our own reactions and responses and their effects on us and on others. In acknowledging those experiences when we feel uncomfortable or elated, subdued or anxious, we become more and more aware of ourselves and what drives our own behaviours and presence. Such enhancement of our antennae and perception provides the ingredients for adventure, seeing the possibilities and richness in the immediacy of the world around us.

Carpe diem? I wish.

Two

Where to begin? I seem to rummage about a lot, earnest but indecisive, stumbling across the clutter of too many false starts. Of course, even as I contemplate this miasma, I have begun again. This time I want to give the exploration more shape and form. The road less travelled is likely to be clear of conceit and sentimentality. These are the black ice of any journey, treacherous because they are deceptive.

For the moment I need to be very still. I want to get it all straight in my head. I lie here a little longer, eyes closed. I aim to move forward as I am, as much as possible stripped of all roles, titles and status. Is this possible? Does life operate at all without the crustation of some label, disguise or manufactured persona? How strangely difficult to conceive of oneself outside of a role. How naked that might feel. But if 'being alive' cannot work in this mode, I suspect that I have a major problem from the outset. If it requires the accretion of accessories, with all their associated posturing and positioning, then I am starting from a shaky foundation.

Each day I awaken into a world of fresh possibilities. I may have parcelled out or pencilled in blocks of notional time in which to take care of prior commitments or routine tasks — but in my head the day can be anything I like. How I approach these tasks, how I perceive the spaces in between, is all down to me.

 *Three*

I was reared on a diet of bright ideas and newly found enthusiasms, less honed by academic rigour than by the excitement of eclectic collision. For those were days of ferment, fuelled by living in a war zone, but all the time anticipating that we were on the threshold of powers and processes that were truly transformational.

I still cling to the little library of texts that I acquired then, seeing them even now as seminal in my own grasp of life and reality. Rollo May, Jean-Paul Sartre, Acharya Vinoba Bhave, Colin Wilson, Carl Rogers, Paul Tillich, Erich Fromm, Maurice Friedman, Martin Buber, Anthony Storr, Alexis de Tocqueville, Viktor Frankl, Irvin Yalom — a tidal force, an ocean of enlightenment, each a wave rolling forward with persuasive power. I was really fortunate. The development team of which I was a member invested heavily in raising our own levels of self knowledge and consciousness before working directly with others. Even so, sometimes our enthusiasm overcame our sense of caution; we distilled practice out from these visions, entering uncharted territory as we experimented (sometimes woefully!) with the next new technique, while gorging ourselves on a rich and unstinting diet of journals and visiting facilitators.

Can this be true? Was this how it was? I do believe so. I guess in my mind I have crammed together influences and events that stretched out over a key decade of research, community and organisational intervention. I know I felt very much alive then.

What was fascinating (in contrast to so much of the surrounding culture) was that there was no dogma to teach. Our own constructs of thinking and belief were continually challenged and exploding; a life dominated by overarching external rules and precepts was to be replaced by the possibility of greater self-determination. It became politically subversive to enable others to enter into their own experiences and the traumas of everyday life and discover new ways of perceiving — and changing — what was happening to themselves and to others.

At the heart of the work was the desire to empower — and that has remained undiminished for me over all the intervening years. Our work was with perception, distortion, reality, delusion, consciousness, empathy, dialogue, the constancy of change, the power of language and the vitality of concept in making sense of the frenetic and duplicitous world around. Even as I write this now I am breathless, reliving the passion of those days.

I find it interesting how so much of what we 'discovered' then seems so commonplace (even common sense!) now:

Disruptive children frequently hit out or walked out because of an absence of language with which to negotiate; the crude distinctions that they made left little space for shades of grey

Issues unresolved in childhood so easily became the bitterness and baggage, stored up and spilling out into extreme adult behaviour

Accusations about past wrongs, and attempts to correct them, had to be accompanied by processes through which people dealt with each other, as they experienced each other, in the live moments of encounter

'Win-win' was a novel negotiating tactic and consensus building was preferable to submission or compromise

Simple disagreements could very quickly spiral into major conflicts when people chose to distance themselves from one another

Many of yesterday's leaders grew tired and entrenched in their views, but couldn't let go, so setting a crippling agenda for a new generation

In essence, in each and every case we were brought back to working with 'reality', or rather the many realities that are at play in any human interaction. Only later did I come to appreciate how problematic it is to stand outside of one's own culture. No doubt, under closer scrutiny, I too was swept away by the easy pull of generalisations, requiring little evidential base or intellectual effort. But these are memories of thirty years ago and, I know, they symbolise a time of great optimism in my life.

My debt is immense. The ideas that governed my work then and ever since largely emanated from that amazing body of writing produced by philosophers, psychotherapists and social analysts in the forty years between the late 1930s and the late 1970s. The Second World War had a huge impact on human consciousness and the subsequent thought and practice of a committed generation was truly transformational. Even as I record these thoughts, I am even more aware of how the existentialist school of that period continues to permeate my mind and spirit and strengthen me in my own battle with illness and loss.

 *Four*

> The ultimate meaning of man's life is not a matter of
> his intellectual cognition but rather the matter of his
> existential commitment.
>
> —Viktor Frankl (6)

I first encountered Viktor Frankl on the wild wind swept
north Antrim coast of N. Ireland, the impact of his writing
as startling and raw as the landscape itself. As an eager
young community worker I became involved in a weekend
reconciliation workshop at a residential centre, perched
on the coastal headland. I recall well the dilapidated
brochure carousel lurching at an odd angle in the corner of
the entrance foyer. Most of the leaflets were bundled and
thumbed and crammed into ill defined sections. There was
just one copy of a rather battered orange booklet, printed
on cheap paper, published by the oddly named 'Better
Yourself Books' and printed in Allahabad, India. How it
had ever arrived there was strange in itself — and I think it
was this incongruity that drew me to it. And then the title,
Man's Search For Meaning: An Introduction to Logotherapy
by Viktor Frankl. In spite of the inauspicious appearance
and presentation it had a preface and introduction by two
distinguished thinkers of the day, Gordon Allport and
Leslie D Weatherhead. I have carried this little text with

me throughout my life ever since. Each reading has moved me yet again, drawn me back to focus on fundamental issues of human understanding with fresh revelations about myself as I experience my own periods of illness, crisis and despair.

Frankl described the horrors of being an inmate in Auschwitz concentration camp and what he discovered there about survival. This, in turn, became the basis of Logotherapy, his particular approach to psychiatry. He held profound and challenging views on perception, personal responsibility, freedom, self transcendence and the primary force of meaning in our mental health. He was fond of quoting Nietzsche: 'He who has a why to live can bear with almost any how'.

It was Frankl who really opened the door for me into existentialism. It was he who jolted me into awareness of the existential vacuum that exists in so many lives. His response to that vacuum was to urge a therapeutic focus on meaning in life. He cautioned that one should not search for an abstract meaning as if handed down to us from somewhere outside ourselves, but rather 'each man is questioned by life; and he can only answer to life by answering for his own life'. (7)

For Frankl that definition of life embraced death and suffering as intrinsic: 'If there is a meaning in life at all, then there must be a meaning in suffering. Suffering is an ineradicable part of life, even as fate and death. Without suffering and death, human life cannot be complete. . . .

The way we bear suffering is a testament to the last inner freedom'. (8)

This last freedom, he asserted, was all to do with choosing one's attitude in any given set of circumstances. A younger contemporary of Frankl, Rollo May, put it this way in his book *Man's Search for Himself:* 'Whether he has tuberculosis or is a slave like the Roman philosopher, Epicletus, or a prisoner condemned to death, he can still in his freedom choose how he will relate to these facts'. (9)

So the opportunity arose to discover in ourselves moral strengths such as braveness, dignity and unselfishness. 'Everywhere', said Frankl, 'man is confronted with fate, with the chance of achieving something through his own suffering'. (10)

After all these years enthusing to others about Viktor Frankl's ideas, only just now do I begin to understand what he meant. It dawns on me with every morning's waking pain. To know 'about' an idea is one thing; to have internalised it and committed oneself not only intellectually but also emotionally and psychologically is quite another.

 *Five*

To-day I seemed unable to summon a coherent thought. Everything was in an untidy jumble, a nervy jingle jangle in my head, like some gigantic reverberating noise, upending my equilibrium. I couldn't hold on to an idea or make cohesion of the streams of disconnected words and images that bounced through my brain and threw my feelings into disarray. I was completely at sea. Now, I am exhausted with pain and so, so tired of feeling sick. Every bone and joint aches. I am restless and irritable.

Chronic illness is such a ghastly, indeterminate affliction. Most perplexing is the inability to 'locate' oneself on any measure of wellness or sickness, living or dying. I now know just how crucial are benchmarks for everyday living. They are the compass and map on which we gauge our progress along any path, whether that is the quality of our relationships or the effectiveness of our actions and decisions. When there is no benchmark, no clear indicator of where we are or how well we are doing, life takes on the character of what Frankl described as a 'provisional existence without limit'. (11) No one can tell me much about how the disease will proceed or what my life expectancy might reasonably be. I seem to be in uncharted territory, not able to plan except for the day I am in.

A cancer patient that I met, who talked about getting rid of a lot of the 'stuff' he had accumulated over many years of professional practice, had a desire to paint again. On his better days he thought how good it would be to convert his former office into a studio. Week after week he procrastinated, eventually saying to me 'but I don't know how long I have'. In truth everyone on the planet could say this — but it doesn't paralyse them from action or fulfilment. The limbo state of critical or chronic illness so easily becomes a barren desert, where no commitment seems possible. That is part of the illness, an intrinsic wound in the suffering.

The choice remains: do I die a little more each day or live life that bit more abundantly?

Six

Sometimes it is easier to describe experiences in their
negative before one is able to recognise what they might
mean in positive terms. Possessing 'a sense of self' is
a useful example — in other words to describe the
experience of losing one's sense of self greatly sharpens and
enhances our image of what it might have been in the first
place. There are some things, like a sense of self, that we
take for granted, as part of our ontological condition, that
are 'there' and 'fundamental', almost pre-conditional, but
slightly beyond our grasp to specify until they all unravel
or fall apart.

The words that follow are a painful and inadequate
attempt to describe the actual experience of loss and
disintegration that I felt when I was extremely ill and, as it
turned out, close to dying. The unravelling that took place
was violent and rapid; the accompanying mental disarray,
shocking. I experienced a frightening loss of control over
many aspects of my existence. I had become so physically
depleted and emaciated that I felt entirely dependant and
incapable of making decisions for myself. I lost any sense
of future and, worse, could retrieve very little of the past,
since my life to that point seemed to have shattered and
fragmented into an incoherent tangle.

This was not purely a fault with my memory; rather it was an extraordinary and distressing inability on my part to form cohesive pictures or any pattern of significance in my life. I was beset by anxiety about trivialities. I was gripped by panic and irrational fears; most bizarrely, distorted memories and dreams shot to the surface, twisting the truth (as it seemed to me) out of all recognition. All of the tools that had served me well in the past, which I had used to affirm myself, to maintain a strong image of who I was or what I could do, that gave a distinctive identity and sense of self, now seemed to fail me.

The collateral damage to my partner and family was immense. Their anguish, fear, insecurity and deep, deep weariness is not accounted for so readily or apparently. All the time, out of love, from their deepest reserves, they found the positive energy to encourage, to support, to hold together the disintegrating fabric of their own lives. Lying in the hospital bed, I felt powerless. It is one of the most upsetting experiences of my life to witness how the person I loved the most became the victim and prisoner of my own plight.

Only very, very slowly, as my physical health returned, was I able to claw my way out and piece together a picture of what I had become — for in truth, there was no way back to what I had been. And all of this was compounded by what I perceived to be other people's reactions to me. For some, with whom I had many and frequent dealings, I was out of circulation and to all intents and purposes had become 'invisible'. Contact suddenly ceased. I was no longer a player on their stage. Many did maintain contact but I sensed that they no longer engaged with me as someone who was a necessary part of the cut and thrust of the world they were in, but as someone who was removed from that world, isolated by illness.

As I began to gather some strength, I wrote

These days I am short of breath and susceptible to sad music. If I tell you my story you will judge me hopelessly melancholic. And because I do not want you to think of me this way, I may never tell you, and you will never really know me.

I am etched in at the margins of everything; there seems no way back. The view from the circumference is satisfying so long as I do not crave belonging. I comprehend the world with uncomfortable perspicacity, sometimes blunted, perverse but inexorably myopic. To say I feel diminished is to say nothing.

Reading this now I am aware of the level of self pity that comes across — but I think it is sufficiently important and truthful to include. For the first time in my life I have a real sense of what it is to lose that sense of self and, conversely, to deeply appreciate what it might be 'to have it' and to nurture it. Hegel said that human beings exist 'only in being acknowledged'. He's talking about life, not existence. Anthony Storr writes: 'Self realisation is not an anti-social principle; it is firmly based on the fact that men need each other in order to be themselves, and that those people who succeed in achieving the greatest degree of independence and maturity are also those who have the most satisfying relationships with others'. (12)

So it is that new sets of relationships have to be built, far away from the instrumentality of working life.

Jung's definition of the cohesive personality gives a clue as to how I imagined I was before being ill — and most certainly how I want to be now. 'Personality is the supreme realisation of the innate idiosyncrasy of a living being. It is an act of high courage flung in the face of life, the absolute affirmation of all that constitutes the individual, the most successful adaptation to the universal conditions of existence coupled with the greatest possible freedom for self-determination'. (13)

Such freedom will require a newly found confidence within and about myself. I don't want to assume anything any more — or conform or adhere to anything that feels incongruent in any way. It will also mean being with others in a different way. This will take work and time, and a commitment to living out in practice the choices and values that I hold in my head.

℞ Seven

> The essential transitoriness of human existence adds to life's meaningfulness. If man were immortal, he would be justified in delaying everything; there would be no need to do anything right now. Only under the urge and pressure of life's transience does it make sense to use the passing time.
>
> —Viktor Frankl (14)

This proposition seems entirely optimistic to me. It suggests that we strongly locate ourselves around one of the very few points of certainty in our existence — and offers a realistic context and a liberating perspective for everything that precedes death. In doing so, it induces an existentialist perspective, optimising on the possibilities in each moment; death's imminence and terminality mean we can be released should those moments prove too burdensome.

But of course, arriving at such clear-headed commitment is far from straightforward. I have read sufficiently in the traditions of western philosophy to appreciate that, over centuries, thinkers broadly came to the same conclusion — that if death can be seen as a helpful empowerment of life then much of our feelings of personal angst are reduced or removed. However, I am aware from my own situation, and through talking with others in the same boat, of just how many find it very hard to put into words the deep unease that they experience when faced with death's closeness and inevitability.

In his landmark text, *Existential Psychotherapy*, Irvin Yalom seems to me to have acutely observed what is at play in this mysterious, often dreadful, existential vacuum. He captures and describes, clearly and cogently, the extraordinary floating anxieties that most of us encounter at the more testing moments in our lives. (A musical parallel would be Henryk Górecki's 3rd Symphony which gives voice, so potently and eloquently, to our deepest pangs of loss and suffering.) Drawing from various psychopathologies encountered in his consulting rooms, Yalom builds a thesis that has equal import for those who are beset by the turbulence which surfaces in illness, when defences are down.

He describes the 'conflict that flows from the individual's confrontation with the givens (ultimate concerns) of existence'. (15) These ultimate concerns are death (a dark unsettling presence at the rim of consciousness), freedom (with its terrifying implication of our own entire responsibility for how we handle life), isolation (each of us enters existence alone and must depart it alone) and meaninglessness (if there is no preordained design then each of us must construct our own meaning in life).

These are the primal, underpinning forces that operate under the surface of all our lives, pushed down and out of sight because of their intense discomfort but lurking, ready to confront us, when the chips are down. They are, however, supremely important in that they ask of us to be fully mature and accepting of reality. How we would long for it not to be so, how we cry out for someone else to take responsibility, to shoulder the weight, to help with the choices, to reassure us that there is some ultimate direction and purpose.

I refer to this paradigm because it has struck me time and again how little we are prepared in our upbringing or education (state or religious) to comprehend any of these fundamental forces that produce such pain when we hit the rocks. At that point, there are so many things that we just cannot do any more — yet we cling to them as if for self preservation.

Yalom regularly tested structured 'disidentification' exercises to help individuals strip away those layers of superficial preoccupation that block attentiveness to the real issues at play in our lives and prevent us from reaching the centre of a 'purer consciousness' (in my terms a more authentic sense of self). This involves the systematic shedding of attributes that we cling to, thinking that our very existence depends on them, but that we can no longer sustain because of our illness or mental condition. These could include elements as diverse as our career, our personal physical attractiveness, our capacity to care for someone else, our ability to make a living or to be an effective parent.

In case after case of chronic and critical illness it became clear to Yalom that we have to let go of these; it's almost as if the very attributes that we build our success on can come back to haunt us because they can no longer be a part of who we are becoming. This involves a journey of acceptance — and that can be slow and traumatic. The acceptance, however, is not only of what we cannot do but, even more importantly, of the maturity asked of us in the paradigm.

As we attain a courage and ability to be free and unafraid, we learn to build new lives within our new capacities, with choices based on meaning that we determine for ourselves. Yalom refers to cancer patients who, when expressing what they had learned from their confrontation with death, lamented 'What a tragedy that we had to wait 'til now, 'til our bodies were riddled with cancer, to learn these truths'! (16)

Consciousness of the inevitability of death helps me cope with the loss inherent in life. The inevitability directs the emphasis on to valuing the actual moment of engagement with others rather than some kind of desperate clinging to the idea that they will be permanently available. Coping with loss helps me grow up. Naïvety and sentimentality are replaced by respect and estimation; possessiveness and acquisition traded for a life with less baggage. I hope.

In so far as decay and departure pervade everything around, I want to recognise the desirability of this and align myself with the promise of renewal that exists in the demise of 'things'. I anticipate and welcome ageing and the opportunity it gives to make sense of what I have already encountered. I am enjoying removing myself from seeming to need so much.

 *Eight*

God enters the arena of sickness. At first he comes gently in the messages from friends and acquaintances of all faiths that they are 'praying for me'. He comes more persistently, knocking on the threshold of my upbringing and conscience. I attend worship in the Hospice and hear the quiet reassurance of familiar words and liturgy. I am moved to tears. But why?

I sense the quickening tension within between reason in the one corner and faith in the other. The sparring begins in my head.

Why am I alive? How did I survive? Was it down to the prayers so earnestly offered by so many people? Was God moved to pity and swayed by the persistence and intensity of their requests? But is God so fickle? Would I have died if they hadn't prayed? Would it have made any difference if there had only been one prayer? Can God's mind be changed or softened or made more malleable? I can't imagine this is so. Had I died what then the efficacy of all these prayers? Would that have been rationalised away as 'God's will'? What an unseemly logic — he can't lose, can he?

If one claims that God 'intervenes' in the planet, or in

individual lives, then logically the same God 'chooses' not to intervene and all the pain, suffering, and disaster that beset the innocent of this world beg a better explanation. This is no light-hearted or cynical dismissal of the concern of others. It confronts me again to be honest about the experience of illness. The assumption of an external entity sits uneasily; that this entity chooses (or not) to intervene in the progress of our lives seems very far from the reality of existence.

I am much more interested in the actual experience which flowed from suffering, demanding a reappraisal of the life lived and the life left. I found it (and continue to find it) most intriguing to realise that the qualities I yearned for in myself were precisely the attributes of God: love, patience, graciousness, creative power, generosity, justice, mercy, forgiveness, wisdom. It seemed that only in accessing these within my day to day life could I begin to feel 'worthy of my suffering' and be the person I wanted to be. Not so long ago Rabbi Lionel Blue wrote in the *Independent* newspaper: 'If the kingdom of heaven is within you, then you can't know about God without knowing about yourself; if you try you'll end up in fanaticism or banality'.

Illness has brought home to me more forcefully than ever how much of my mental and emotional energy had at times been directed in wasteful and self-destructive ways. Arrogance, resentment, ill tempered impatience and envy, far from accomplishing anything externally, only served to punish and harm myself. Deepak Chopra in his book *Journey Into Healing* quotes an old Indian saying 'If you want to see what your thoughts were like yesterday, look at your body to-day. If you want to see what your body will be like tomorrow, look at your thoughts to-day'. (17) I guess I've done a lot of damage to myself over the years!

We are told that man is made in the 'image of God'. It's a powerful way to put it — the core of who we are yearns to be whole and well by authentically giving life to the attributes listed above. For me, this is the spirit of life, offering a transcendent and spiritually healthy way to be. I have witnessed this extraordinary vitality time after time in those who are suffering and put me to shame. It seems to me the 'attributes of God' are potentialities in every human being, but so often (I see it in myself) obscured, obstructed, drowned out by the busy clamour of life or the noise of ephemeral, immediate and superficial satisfactions. They come as gift but have to be chosen, released to be free within us, to fill up the existential vacuum of our lives. Kierkegaard wrote in his epilogue to *Fear and Trembling: The Sickness Unto Death*: 'Whatever the one generation may learn from the other, that which is genuinely human no generation learns from the foregoing . . . Thus no generation has learned from another to love, no generation begins at any other point than at the beginning'. (18)

 Nine

It appears that my energy levels are not only enhanced by positive thought but, even more so, by my ability to construct adventures for the mind. For much of my life I have very much enjoyed discovering new places, new spaces. I have travelled far and been filled with delight and wonder at the extraordinary differences, the immense beauty, the sensory richness of cultures and their expressions.

Sometimes even the appalling squalor, deprivation and inhumanity seemed to merge into the awesome nature of what I was seeing. More than once I have had to remind myself that I should not slip into the detachment of a voyeur but understand that I am part of this landscape and it is but a mirror on to huge injustice and violation of basic human rights. As part of this world I am responsible. Most significantly, the me that is in everything I encounter determines the existential quality and truth of the experience.

Now deprived of that travel, I still am driven to make my own journeys. I need to breathe easily, to have a physical, and metaphysical, sensation of space, wide open horizons stretching before me. Since I don't live in an Idyll

— the sky is not unbounded blue every morning — I am determined to construct the reality I move in.

Being alive is the most consummately absorbing occupation and conundrum I can imagine; so I am part of that landscape and contribute to it by choosing how to see it. Recently I have taken to re-evaluating the familiar, all its sensory qualities enlivened, tingling . . . I could go anywhere but I choose to be here because I am discovering how much I haven't seen before.

Antoine de Saint-Exupéry wrote in his beautiful *Flight to Arras:* 'There is a cheap literature that speaks to us of the need of escape. It is true that when we travel we are in search of distance. But distance is not to be found. It melts away. And escape has never led anywhere. The moment a man finds that he must play the races, go to the Arctic, or make war in order to feel himself alive, that man has begun to spin the strands that bind him to other men and to the world. But what wretched strands! A civilisation that is really strong fills man to the brim, though he never stirs. What are we worth when motionless, is the question'. (19)

Reflecting further on what he described as 'density of being' he said, 'Cézanne, mute and motionless before his sketch, is an inestimable presence. He is never more alive than when silent, when feeling and pondering. At the moment his canvas becomes for him something wider than the seas'. (20)

Examples such as Cézanne may seem to be about exceptional people. That need not be so, for there can be absorption in the ordinary that becomes special to each of us, for each his own epiphany.

It would be wrong to imply that Saint-Exupéry in any way dismissed the exploration by man of his universe. His own life speaks volumes about his own passion for adventure. But he is talking about different universes and the vain attempts that we sometimes (often?) make to run away from ourselves. Distraction, in the end, will leave us empty and anxious. I know now how really tough is the journey to find oneself. Perhaps the seeker cannot be the sought. But one has a better chance when there is some perspective, some distance, and some relativity.

In illness, one (I, me) gets a lot of things out of all proportion. There can be huge distortion — and this is as painful for those around the sick person as it is for the person who is ill. Finding one's centre actually means being 'grounded', wisely and properly able to see ourselves in relation to everything else. We become healthier when we stop being the centre of the universe and are able to calmly enter the universe of others with an open, listening and generous spirit. The centred self is very, very different from being self-centred.

What we are worth when motionless? Yes, that's the question.

Ten

Before encountering the hospice, only once in eight years did a doctor ask me — 'And how is your wife coping with your illness'? I was so taken aback by the question that I hastily responded 'Fine, thank you, just fine'.

Fine indeed. Living with, caring for, someone who is critically or chronically ill is much discussed in today's media but, I believe, remains little understood. It may seem contradictory but, as long as the treatment of illness remains so completely and disproportionately focussed on the patient, there will be little relief for those who suffer as a consequence. Support for carers may be increasingly available, but it tends to be concentrated around a small number of high profile conditions (e.g. cancer, MS, HIV AIDS) and is often based on the assumption that the carers will be from an older generation.

We would be wrong if we failed to recognise that there are a significant number of individual non-professional carers who live their lives in a state of limbo, largely unsupported, unless they make extraordinary efforts on their own to seek help. For if you are the partner, parent or child of someone who suffers with a chronic or life threatening illness outside the high profile categories then, largely, you are destined to struggle on your own. Yes, there is a gradual and welcome improvement in the availability of respite care; yes, carers' associations do their best, offering 'away days', 'pamper days', advice and a chance to talk with others in the same boat — but so often the trouble is that you simply cannot 'get away' — especially if you have become the main or only bread winner and have to continue to provide care around the clock while earning a living.

In so many ways, it is assumed that the carer will and can shoulder the burden. Yet, the carer can be cast as peripheral to the professional, there to answer questions, someone to 'take from' rather than be given to. The system, inadvertently, has a powerful capacity to disempower and diminish, whether in the endless waiting, the paucity of information, or the constant repetition of the same questions from various professionals who never seem to pass on the answers to anyone else.

Meanwhile, through the long hours at home, the carer is the constant watcher, carrying the unending anxiety that permeates every waiting and waking moment. For many, there is no escape, not in the hallway or the kitchen, not in the study or the sitting room. The house takes on an eerie weariness. There is no spring in the stair or much light from the windows. It's like its very soul has succumbed as a witness to dread. Am I being too melodramatic? I don't think so; check out the reality with those who live with someone who is chronically ill and face a dreadful indeterminate future.

Paradoxically, the help that is available has its own potential downside, for the carer has to 'let go' of her* private space. What was private becomes public as one admits agency carers or other family members in to help out during the critical peaks and troughs. It may seem trivial, but in such exposed circumstances the principal carer so easily becomes sensitive to any implied judgements (intended or unintended) about how she is coping — and finds difficulty in securing any space and privacy for herself.

Carers regularly describe the constant tension between the physical and emotional aspects of caring. There are a host of practical support needs but here I want to focus on what happens within the carer her (or him) self. I sense that there may be four key painful areas of loss that have to be carried by carers alongside the actual physical and emotional support for their loved one. Each has a cutting edge, each carving away another part of the life that one imagined one had before illness struck.

Firstly, there is the loss of a functioning partner. In life we commit to companions who play complementary roles within our lives; so we help to fulfil each other, bring completeness or add uniqueness. Suddenly, crippling illness and incapacity remove ingredients that we need or have come to depend on from our partner. This may mean that we lose our lover, we lose our protector. We have to

---

*References to the carer as female in this essay are personal and are not intended to exclude male carers.

take control and responsibility for so much that we were formerly able to leave to that 'other part of ourselves'.

In practice there is little warning about the levels of emotional stamina required or of the extremes and stages that the emotions go through as illness progresses over a long period. Carers can find themselves feeling guilty about some of the feelings they experience; this intensifies their sense of not coping. A carer's desire to make a positive contribution so often depends on how the patient copes with his or her own illness; if there are signs of improvement or recognition, the carer is able to feel she is making a difference; when there is no positive feedback she has no benchmarks against which to place value on all her effort. So, in the dynamic between carer and patient, the one can drag the other down.

Secondly, there is the loss of a personal life. The demands of care mean sacrifice. We have to change arrangements, let other people down. We have to negotiate our way into new working patterns that often may cause disruption or added pressure for others. We become cautious of making any commitments and, as a consequence, gradually cease to be a part of other people's plans. Our former identity and sense of direction has to be subsumed under the guise of carer — and we may even resent this and find the new role uncomfortable, however much we love our partner. There can be an extraordinary conflict between how society values individuals and how the carer maintains any self-esteem.

In a world where so much emphasis is given to success and attainment, placing immense energy into the invisible caring role, particularly where 'things just aren't going to get any better', can be very painful. It is hard to avoid the feeling that life is passing you by — particularly when you are still relatively young; that the equivalent energy could have been directed into embarking on new adventures, making a wonderful piece of art or into becoming a successful business woman. Yet so much energy seems drained into something where there is little externally valued sense of recognition. In caring, one opts for a role for which there is no training, no income and no obvious reward. Because you now know how bad it can get, you can become quite fearful for your own future.

Thirdly, there is the loss of life before death. There is tremendous pain in being a witness to the real 'absence' of a viable life before the inevitable death takes place. This is the limbo world, in which one clings to signs of life while only recognising signs of dying. So often unacknowledged in the conscious mind, this distress inhabits our subconscious life, and can unleash all kinds of unnamed angst and dread. Indeed, there may even be long term damage, not apparent in the present, from the suppression of such prolonged intense anxiety.

Here the most agonising dilemmas may have to be confronted. To perform 'the role' effectively, the carer may have to achieve some emotional distance. In turn, that may mean having to 'let go' of the person she loves, to set aside the fact that one is caring for someone with whom there is another deep relationship. It is painfully hard to watch someone whom you love slowly degenerate knowing that there is little you can do to help.

Finally, there is a loss of a hoped for future. When life is on hold for a long time or where the prospect is one of a journey without the companion we love, so many of our aspirations have to be let go also. This may even mean the end of a career or the annihilation of our economic security. It may face us with a struggle for which we feel decidedly unprepared and ill equipped. It may blight the possibility of adventure or personal fulfilment in areas of our lives that we had previously valued as fundamental to our vision of happiness.

Carers express a deep 'sadness' about how the sense of living with illness seems to pervade everything — and how so easily they can construct a sense of their own future that envisages a transition from caring into coping with their own ageing and, perhaps illness, alone. Prolonged chronic illness by nature is indeterminate, leading into a future with no map, few benchmarks and little possibility of remission. It produces what Viktor Frankl called 'a provisional existence without limit'. For the carer, that may be the ultimate price to pay.

So, there is a cutting edge to care. These four losses may not be the same for everyone — and without doubt, many carers will testify to the rediscovered values and richness that they have experienced in giving of themselves in such a way to another human being. But if there is any truth in what is described above then I suspect there needs to be some reappraisal of what we mean by 'the support of carers'. In particular, I could not find any carer who had been warned about what might happen — or given any preparation for the weight he/she was expected to carry.

Illness is not 'one thing'; it is not a single homogenous entity. Coping with a serious degenerative illness is a very different proposition from coping with something acute — where there is a critical, frightening time, perhaps risky surgery, but where there is recovery and moving on. The latter, for the carer, at least includes the opportunity of a 'rebirth', where there is the prospect of rebuilding and growing not only as an individual but in the relationship. Long, slow degenerative illness (and often associated depression) does not offer such a prospect but instead offers increasing invisibility and loss of self, unless very determined and courageous choices are made by the carer for herself.

Support, in whatever way it is given, can never take away the reality that society depends hugely on family or companions to carry the weight of caring for each other. That probably is as it should be. But equally the reality is that critical or serious degenerative chronic illnesses are not the domain of the sick person alone. There is much hidden collateral damage. It is probably unrealistic to expect the medical diagnostic process to incorporate (proactively and comprehensively) an assessment of the implications for the carer. But it may be valid to ask whether or not more could be done to put in place structures, processes and people capable of understanding and supporting the carer through such inherent loss.

There seems to be no obvious paradigm through which carers can guide themselves through the tumultuous upheavals that go with the role. Perhaps these thoughts imply that a non-ageist survival guide for carers is desperately needed.

 *Eleven*

In the self-help industry of literature there is repeated admonition to develop daily disciplines and choose pathways that lead us into contact with others. So we are encouraged to create structures of routine that help impel us through those moments of heaviness or dullness. We are persuaded to take initiatives which hook us into other people's already existing social networks — clubs, societies, adult education classes, group recreations — all facilitating exchange and the possibility of being drawn forward by the energy and ideas of others. Consequently, we don't have to find or invent all these processes on our own. And such homely wisdom derives from sound pedigree. Sartre was cautious of the developing fashion for going inward (introspection) and suggested that we only truly find ourselves when we move out from ourselves into experiences with others and in that very alive dynamic we discover, learn, renew and take pleasure.

I have found that the most potent of the simple self-help rules is the commitment to achieving at least one new initiative each day — to accomplish something, however small, that did not exist at the outset of the day. Perhaps it is to get up out of bed and have a wash, no matter how long this may take, with no matter how many intermittent rest breaks. Perhaps it is to write a paragraph of a long waiting letter or article; perhaps it is to record a single important thought so that it does not slip away; or read the next chapter of a book. Perhaps it is to extend the length of a daily walk or take over the preparation of a meal for which you had previously been dependent on someone else. Perhaps it is to contact someone who is lonely or repair a neglected relationship. In that way our progress, our sense of self achievement and the worthwhileness of the day become manifest. It would seem that such affirmation is a tonic, a key building block to rebuilding our will and confidence and motivation.

And yet I am amazed at a bizarre twist that I discover in all these conquests; having made immense effort, they all seem so very little, so ordinary. Perhaps that is their ultimate value in that they create the semblance of normality — and how welcome that ordinariness is. But it is then that I experience a horror of other people's misplaced effusive remarks that seem to imply I have done something 'heroic' in taking each small step. I recoil; they don't know it but they make me feel pathetic.

Viktor Frankl wrote: 'I consider it a dangerous misconception of mental hygiene to assume that what man needs in the first place is equilibrium or, as it is called in biology, 'homeostasis', i.e. a tensionless state. What man actually needs is not a tensionless state but rather the striving and struggling for some goal worthy of him. What he needs is not the discharge of tension at any cost, but the call of a potential meaning waiting to be fulfilled by him'. (21)

I am beginning to appreciate that I am evolving again. The little steps, however small, cumulatively and subtly represent a series of choices about how I want to be. Being alive, then, is not about bringing ease, an endless smoothing of the disturbing ripples of life. A core dynamic for mental health is 'the tension between what one has already achieved and what one still ought to accomplish, or the gap between what one is and what one should become'. (22) 'Becoming' provides both the passion and imperative for really sticking at it, for wakening up each new day to see the possibility waiting.

℞ Twelve

I watch a nurse cross the room towards a day care cancer patient. He seems agitated, ill at ease, and uncomfortable in himself. She smiles and checks if he needs anything. He shakes his head. She sits down near to him and expresses interest in where he is from. His eyes catch hers.

She asks a few questions, very few, just enough to connect. A name, a place, a neighbour, his work . . . hesitant at first, then a gentle cadence creeps into the conversation. His life story begins to unfold, to ebb and flow, first a rush of words, then a long silence. She takes disjointed bits and pieces from him and carefully hands them back with shape and form. She jogs his memory, shares in his delights and his misfortunes. There is something of pain, something of loss. Occasionally there are little ripples of laughter and odd whispered indiscretions. All the time she holds him in the embrace of her total attentiveness.

Almost 40 minutes on, she eases back, he is nodding, relaxed. As she rises it's like his spirit moves upwards with her. She is magnificent. She is emotionally drained; she has given of herself completely.

This is St. John's Hospice at work.

The best, perhaps the only, institution that I have come across with any real insight into the treatment of illness 'in the round' is the hospice. It is certainly the case that its structure, resourcing, medical model, philosophy of care and staff-patient ratios are all significantly different from the average hospital, so enabling it to deliver a more holistic approach. The dictionary defines 'palliative' as 'serving to cloak or conceal; serving to relieve (disease) superficially or temporarily, or to mitigate pain'. I have come to appreciate that this is an entirely inadequate term to describe what happens in a hospice. Of course at its core there is a tremendously detailed and methodical attention to finding the right drug combinations to ameliorate the intense nausea and pain suffered by patients. There is highly effective communication between the different types of professional staff, between shifts and between staff, patients and their families. All of this is accomplished with immense discretion, dignity and respect for privacy.

Staff have time for patients. They listen. They facilitate the expression of worries and concerns, and then help patients or families explore how best to deal with these. They grasp (innately or through training?) that they cannot achieve a physical improvement without building the will, confidence, perspective and courage of each individual. They are 'hands on'. So whether it is blood transfusions, wound dressing, physiotherapy, medication management, feeding, bathing, changing, dressing or taking you out to the garden for your first breath of fresh air in days — all are accomplished with an eye to how one intervention may impact another, how the total is more than the sum of the parts. You may engage in the most helpful, encouraging conversation while having your toe nails clipped!

I only know all this because I have experienced it at first hand. For me, and for many others, hospice is not just a place that handles death; it is a place that gives you life. During my time as a patient I have tried to understand what the process is that makes such a difference. I don't need any more evidence to tell me that there is an actual dynamic link between our state of mind (and spirit) and our ability to cope with chronic or critical illness.

Universities in the States, Europe and Japan are producing more and more studies to demonstrate how 'psychosocial variables' can affect conditions as diverse as cardiovascular disease, cancer and irritable bowel syndrome — and, hence, survival. My own encounter with the Hospice reminded me of a little reported piece of research conducted at Harvard University by Theodore A. Kotchen, published in the *Journal of Individual Psychology* in 1960. In his article, 'Existential Mental Health: an Empirical Approach', Kotchen identified seven traits which, on testing, appeared most pertinent to mental health. The traits are — uniqueness, responsibility, self-affirmation, courage, transcendence, faith-commitment and world view. (23) Of course each has a very specific definition and set of indicators (largely based on the work of existentialist thinkers and therapists such as Frankl, Rollo May, Tillich and Kierkegaard). Together, in Kotchen's estimate, they constitute the core force of 'meaningfulness' in life — and their absence, even partial, leads to anxiety, despair and distortion of reality.

Experience tells me that these are an intrinsic part of the landscape on which illness has its battleground. The struggle to be 'alive', rather than just to exist, requires that we conquer the distress and despair engendered when our whole sense of self and meaningfulness are under threat. At its best, palliative care joins in that battle. It works assiduously to offer the best shot at life, the best quality of life possible, by skilfully blending physical and medical treatment regimes with careful work to restore the shattered self.

So much of this is both elementary and profound. It is almost impossible to rediscover our sense of significance and value or face regrets or deal with unfinished business when we are retching and vomiting or twisted with pain. But when we are helped to find our courage perhaps we also change the bio-chemical potential for healing and the prolonging of life. Of course nothing cancels death. Most people just want to be more ready to meet it. It is on this ground that the physical, mental, emotional and spiritual meet. The existential vacuum of Yalom is no less to do with the physical than physiotherapy is divorced from the mind and will.

𝌆 *Endpiece*

I have learned that absolutes provide a comforting illusion of permanence and certainty but dissolve in the face of my aloneness. Arguably, the biggest culprit in our language is the word 'is'. Think about it. So many of our certainties and neat little distinctions are securely carved on our consciousness by the word 'is'. That's it, wrapped up, sorted! That tiny word is so definite, so complete and so sure. It is so lacking in partiality or ambiguity. It gives us reality the way we want it, devoid of paradoxical discomfort. But it nestles with explosive potential in the midst of our well ordered constructs or manicured perspectives. All too readily it becomes what it is not.

I think that 'being alive' means letting go of such shackles. I know I'll find that challenging, for I have loved my certitude! So I developed a little mantra to help me along the way.

I need to

Live life with a consciousness of death
Live life with a realistic sense of my
    portion in time and history

Live life in each moment fully, rather
than pass through
Live life free of fear
Live life in the consciousness of possibility
Live life with a sense of humour
Live life with an awareness for my
propensity towards delusion
Live life with an awareness of the values
implicit in my behaviour and passions
Live life at all times open to the possibility
that I may be wrong
Live life free from an excess of absolutes
Live life conscious of anger as an emotional
register of my own insufficiency
Live life in other peoples' shoes
Live each day and situation
with personal responsibility
Live life in the knowledge that
ultimately I am on my own
Live life in the consciousness that the more I move
out from myself into the universe of others, the
more I will find chords that echo and reassure.

I have arrived at a quiet place. In the past such stillness
was unnerving and disturbingly empty. Into that vacuum
would rush the demons of disconcerting thoughts and
spiralling, ill defined anxiety. It was so much easier to fill
up life with earnest doing and blot out silence with the

noise of occupation and propulsion into the next bright idea.

But now I have settled into the quiet. Surprisingly it is far from vacuous. At last I can listen to the rhythm of my own life; because there is no longer an aggravating urgency, I begin to hear other voices, other sentiments. Because there is nothing to sell, no agenda, no ulterior motive, there is an amazing amount of space within which I can better hear what others might wish to communicate. Conversations become less fleeting, more meaningful; looks exchanged, more knowing. Time is less wasted on trivialities. Joy is more frequently revealed in the little things of life that really are enormously significant in that incredible universe that each of us weaves as we make and remake our personal and family stories. Faced with the ultimate brevity of life, I have discovered how vast the volume of time is in each moment. And in this quiet I find a peace that I have not known before.

David, the chaplain, speaks of the Beatitudes. They seem contradictory, implausible, derisory. I shake my head; I want to turn my mind away. But I am drawn to their directness. Their voice is for those who mourn. They call out to those whose spirits are squashed, who are cornered, afflicted and assaulted with the worst that the world can throw at them. Their promise seems impossible, almost ineffable. Yet, being alive, I know they are real.

As with wise men, he shows no surprise at the enormity of the ideas — just a simple acceptance grounded in his own tried and tested experience. As is the way of the hospice, he offers me an arm to lean on, new ground to stand on. There is no naïvety, no pretence. It's about the future, he says, not measured in minutes or months — but in depth, through moments of sheer delight and surprise, discovery and conquest. Go make more memories, he says. I will.

Golden amber and, like myself, drawn firm
to the fits and starts, the harassments of life,
unwavering, constant, with radiant smile
outfacing the shadows that at length must win:
If it spoke it would say: 'I can guess your thoughts:
that fear of extinction has made me weep.
Do not misjudge these tears for grief foreknown,
for the eye may brim with overwhelming mirth'.

—Abu al-Ala al-Maarri
Syria (24)

But often, in the world's most crowded streets,
But often, in the din of strife,
There rises an unspeakable desire
After the knowledge of our buried life,
A thirst to spend our fire and restless force
In tracking out our true, original course;
A longing to inquire
Into the mystery of this heart that beats
So wild, so deep in us, to know
Whence our thoughts come and where they go.

—Matthew Arnold (25)

Notes and references

(1) **Gösta Ågren**, Death's Secret, one of a fine and inspiring collection of poems, *Staying Alive*, edited by Neil Astley, Bloodaxe Books 2002, p. 382

(2) **Louis de Bernières**, *Birds Without Wings*, Vintage 2005 p. 25

(3) **Robert Hobson**, *Forms of Feeling: The Heart of Psychotherapy*, Tavistock/Routledge 1985 p. 224. This theme, repeated throughout the book, culminates in the most clear and powerful way in Chapter 13: Love and Loss

(4) **Thomas Attig**, Relearning the World: Making and Finding Meanings. This is Chapter 2 in a collection edited by Robert A. Neimeyer, *Meaning Reconstruction and the Experience of Loss*, American Psychological Association 2001, pp. 36–38

(5) ibid, p. 48

(6) **Viktor E. Frankl**, *Psychotherapy and Existentialism: Selected Papers on Logotherapy*, Penguin Books 1967, p. 85

(7) **Viktor E. Frankl**, *Man's Search for Meaning: An Introduction to Logotherapy*, Better Yourself Books, Saint Paul Society, Allahabad, India 1977, p. 118

(8) ibid, p. 77

(9) **Rollo May**, *Man's Search for Himself*, Dell Publishing/ Bantam Doubleday 1973, pp. 164–65

(10) **Viktor E. Frankl**, *Man's Search For Meaning*, p. 78

(11) ibid, p. 80

(12) **Anthony Storr**, *The Integrity of the Personality,* Pelican Books 1963, pp. 32–33

(13) **C.G.Jung**, *The Development of Personality,* Routledge and Kegan Paul 1954, p. 171

(14) **Viktor E. Frankl**, *Psychotherapy and Existentialism*, p. 39

(15) **Irvin D. Yalom**, *Existential Psychotherapy,* Basic Books 1980, pp. 8–9

(16) ibid, p.165

(17) **Deepak Chopra**, *Journey Into Healing: Awakening the Wisdom Within You*, Rider/Random House 1995, p. 87

(18) **Søren Kierkegaard**, *Fear and Trembling,* Penguin Books 2003, p. 145

(19) **Antoine de Saint-Exupéry**, *Flight to Arras,* Penguin 1995, p. 53. The text quoted is actually from an earlier translation in 1942 by Lewis Galantieres, but I give the reference to the newer edition because it is readily available.

(20) ibid

(21) **Viktor E. Frankl**, *Man's Search For Meaning,* p. 114

(22) ibid

(23) **Theodore A. Kotchen**, Existential Mental Health: An Empirical Approach, *Journal of Individual Psychology* 1960

(24) **Abu al-Ala al-Maarri**, poem on a candle, from a wonderful collection with a really helpful introduction, in *Classical Arabic Poetry,* translated with an introduction by Charles Greville Tuetey, KPI Limited, Routledge & Kegan Paul plc 1985, p. 270

(25) **Matthew Arnold**, *The Buried Life, Matthew Arnold Poems,* (Internet web site) PoemHunter.com: The World's Poetry Archive 2004, p. 13

Other books that have helped along the way

Jean-Paul Sartre, *Existentialism and Humanism,* Methuen 1989

Maurice Friedman, *To Deny Our Nothingness:Contemporary Images of Man,* Dell Publishing 1967

Colin Wilson, *New Pathways in Psychology,* Victor Gollancz 1973

Walter Kaufmann, *Existentialism, Religion and Death: Thirteen Essays,* Meridian 1976

Sheldon Kopp, *If You Meet the Buddha on the Road, Kill Him,* Sheldon Press 1974

Ben Okri, *A Way of Being Free,* Phoenix 1997

Paul Tillich, *The Courage to Be,* Collins/Fontana 1962

Isaiah Berlin, *Freedom and its Betrayal: Six Enemies of Human Liberty,* Chatto & Windus 2002

A NOTE ON THE AUTHOR

Raymond Johnston was born in Belfast, N.Ireland and lives in England. He was forced to abandon a successful international career in management consultancy when hit by life threatening illness in his early fifties. During the ensuing struggle to survive he discovered the restorative power of memory in helping him build a new life with deeper meaning. *Being Alive* recounts some of the most significant moments of that experience and suggests ways in which those working with the critical or chronically ill can offer life giving support and encouragement.